Look up into the sky. Can you see the rainbow? It arches like a bridge over the hills and comes down into Nutshell Wood. At the end of the rainbow, deep in the wood, a tiny magical village is appearing. That village is Rainbow's End. Rainbow's End can only be seen by humans when a rainbow is in the sky, otherwise it is invisible to everyone except the gnomes who live there and the woodland animals.

The gnomes of Rainbow's End are jolly little folk who are always busy. Lots of exciting and interesting things happen in the village and no one is ever bored. This book tells the story of something that happened there. A little bird told me!

Rainbow's End
Woolly Foot's Good Idea
Written by Jane Patience
Illustrated by John Patience

PUBLISHED BY PETER HADDOCK LIMITED
BRIDLINGTON, ENGLAND
© Rainbow's End Productions

Bristly Oaksbeard was the blacksmith in Rainbow's End and lived with his wife Bryony and their son, Woolly Foot in their home at the base of an oak tree. Many gnomes make their homes in trees and are named after them, too. One morning Bristly was working at his forge. Woolly Foot was working the big bellows to heat up the fire and his father was busy at the anvil, hammering away at a piece of iron to make a new toasting fork for Mrs Hawthorn.

Bryony Oaksbeard came out of the house to say that lunch was ready. All of a sudden, something fluttered by, just over her head, and gave her quite a fright. It was an owl which disappeared into a hole near the top of their oak tree. ''Look, Woolly Foot,'' Bryony said, ''It looks as if we are going to have a new neighbour.'' ''Oh, yes,'' Woolly Foot replied. He thought this was quite exciting and wondered if he would be able to make friends with the owl.

As the weeks went by, Bristly Oaksbeard became more and more bad-tempered. A lot of the other folk noticed this and began to worry about him. "What on earth can be wrong with Bristly these days?" they said. "He's not his usual, cheerful self at all, and do you know what he did yesterday? He actually nodded off to sleep as I was talking to him!" The problem was that the owl who had moved into Bristly's oak tree was keeping him awake all night with her hooting.

One night, as they sat by the crackling fire with steaming mugs of bramble tea and home-made acorn biscuits, Bryony and Bristly were discussing the problem of the owl. What could they do? Woolly Foot appeared at the sitting room door in his pyjamas. "You should be in bed, Woolly Foot," said Bryony. "But I think I can help," replied Woolly Foot. "I have made friends with the owl and she told me that she doesn't like living here herself because your hammering on the anvil keeps her awake all day when she should be asleep." They all decided that the only solution was for Bristly to ask the owl, very politely of course, if she would mind moving to another tree.

The next morning Bristly climbed right up to the owl's nest. The owl opened one eye and looked at him crossly. ''What's this?'' she said. ''You're not satisfied with keeping me awake all day with your silly hammering – now you have climbed up here to disturb me as well.'' Before Bristly knew what was happening she had pushed him out of her nest and he fell down to the ground. Luckily, he landed in a nice soft pile of leaves. Oh dear, now everyone was in a bad mood!

A few days later, Woolly Foot was out collecting berries in the woods when he spied a hole in a tree trunk. Suddenly he had a marvellous idea. If the hole could be made a little bigger, perhaps his friend the owl could be persuaded to live in this tree. Feeling very excited, he rushed home to tell his parents about his idea.

Bryony and Bristly thought it was a wonderful plan. Without wasting any time at all, the town's carpenters, Toddy Meadows and his apprentice Tiny Toadflax, were sent for. Woolly Foot led them through the wood to the tree he had found. Because they usually live in wooded areas where there is plenty of timber, gnomes are very skilful carpenters, so it didn't take Toddy and Tiny long to enlarge the hole in the tree. They made a very neat job of it, too. "There now," said Bristly. "That should be big enough for your owl friend to move into, Woolly Foot." "Yes," the boy replied, "But I just hope she will agree to the plan."

This time Woolly Foot was sent up the tree to talk to the owl. She was pleased to see her young friend and very excited when he told her all about the new home he had found for her. "All right," she said, "I'll have a look at the place, just to see if I like it." So, with Woolly Foot riding on her back to direct her, the owl flew to the new tree, right in the heart of the wood. As soon as she saw it, she fell in love with her new home and settled in happily. That night was very peaceful in Oak Tree House, and in her new home the owl hooted to her heart's content.

RAINBOW'S END